Nicola Jemphrey

Scaldie

First published 2003

ISBN 1 85999 597 7

Scripture Union, 207–209 Queensway, Bletchley, Milton Keynes, MK2 2EB, England.
Email: info@scriptureunion.org.uk
Website: www.scriptureunion.org.uk

Scripture Union Australia
Locked Bag 2, Central Coast Business Centre, NSW 2252
Website: www.su.org.au

British Library Cataloguing-in-Publication Data.
A catalogue record of this book is available from the British Library.

Printed and bound in Great Britain by Creative Print and Design (Wales) Ebbw Vale.

Cover design: Paul Airy

Scripture Union is an international Christian charity working with churches in more than 130 countries, providing resources to bring the good news about Jesus Christ to children, young people and families and to encourage them to develop spiritually through the Bible and prayer.
As well as our network of volunteers, staff and associates who run holidays, church-based events and school Christian groups, we produce a wide range of publications and support those who use our resources through training programmes.

For Alan, Robbie, Erin and Alex, with love.

Chapter 1

A scaldie is a wee bald bird that's fallen out of its nest. Like the one Jules and her dad found while strolling through the school grounds before the summer holidays.

"Poor wee thing," said her dad, burying it under some leaves and soft compost among the roots of the tree. "It hadn't a hope. Not without its mother or anyone else to look after it."

A scaldie is also what Jules's mum called the haircut Chris Jacobs had when he arrived for his first term at Drum Grange Prep School.

That's not what the other boys called it.

"Skinhead!" Jules's mum heard them jeering, as she passed the Common Room on her way home from teaching her evening class. One look at Chris's red eyes and she swept him upwards along with her, through the door of the Housemaster's flat on the top floor and right into their living room.

"Look after Chris for a moment," she hissed at Jules, who was lying on the rug watching football. On her way through to the kitchen she hit the mute button on the remote.

Bad idea.

"That poor wee mite!" Her loudly indignant voice shattered the awkward silence on the other side of the living room wall. "Trust those boys downstairs to pick on someone smaller than themselves. He looks eight, not eleven. Jules is twice the size of him."

Jules and Chris looked at each other, outraged.

"Am not!" said Jules, her blue eyes alight with indignation. She jumped up and they stood back to back in front of the big mirror in the middle of the room.

"See, you're almost as tall as me!" Jules laid one hand flat on her own auburn, curly cropped head and the other on Chris's dark bristly one, then estimated the difference between them. "If your hair was just a few millimetres longer, there'd be nothing in it."

Then a nasty thought struck her.

"Do you suppose she wasn't talking about *height*? I know I eat too much chocolate, but... No, it's you that's too skinny."

Chris couldn't contradict this. Jules's reflection proved nothing more than a healthy appetite, but he looked like a stick insect beside her. His face fell.

"Oh, rats!" said Jules. "That's hardly going to cheer you up, is it? Sit down while I find some tissues. I'm sure there's a new box hidden somewhere."

She crouched down at the end of the room and opened a storage cupboard tucked under the eaves of the school roof. Chris looked on with interest as a strange combination of knitted toys and smelly bottles tumbled out.

"What are all these?" he asked, coming over and picking up a badly stuffed Bob the Builder.

"The fallout from Mum's evening classes,"

Jules replied, still rummaging in the cupboard.

"Huh?"

"From her Knitting for Kids class. Granny nearly had a heart attack when she told her she'd signed up to teach it. Mum hadn't lifted a pair of needles since she was at primary school, but she thought if Granny could do it, there couldn't be much to it." She pulled out a lopsided penguin. "How wrong can you be?"

"And the bottles?"

"Understanding Aromatherapy. Problem was I don't think she ever really did. No one could stand the sort of smells she produced when she was practising at home. Dad and I had to have all our meals downstairs with the boarders. Then one day the Head had a word with Dad. He'd been showing some boys and their parents around the dorms when a mixture of Bog Myrtle and Wildest Lavender oils hit them on the landing. It didn't quite fit the image of a mainly rugby-playing boys' school, he said. So that was that."

"What does your mum do now, then?"

"She went back to teaching Geography. She's good at that. Here, I've found the tissues."

"Don't need them any more," said Chris. "You mean, no one wants this?" He was holding a very un-menacing looking black and red striped Dennis.

"No. You can have it if you like. I've got a whole pile Granny made me in my room. But – I didn't think boys were into cuddly toys. Only the youngest boarders bring any to school – the seven year olds who've just left home."

"I didn't have any when I was that age. Nearly all Mum's friends are in the army. When I was small,

all I was given to play with were toy tanks and soldiers. I hated them."

"Didn't you tell your mum?"

"I couldn't. My dad had been a soldier. He was killed in action when I was only two. I don't remember him at all, but everyone said he was a hero. I thought I should try to become a soldier too."

Chris was looking sad again.

"I could keep Dennis up here for you," Jules suggested. "Then you could always come up if you felt like a cuddle. Not with me," she added hastily.

Chris's pale, thin face broke into a wide smile. "Thanks, I might. Maybe best not to let the other boys see him."

"Were they bullying you?"

"Just laughing at my hair. Especially that big guy, Gareth someone."

"Oh, Gareth Ramsay; surprise, surprise! They're just jealous, you know."

Chris looked incredulous. "Of my hair?"

"Of course! They'd all like to look ultra cool like the footballers. Is yours a number one?"

"No, it's a half. All the men we know in the army keep their hair really short."

"There you are then," Jules said triumphantly. "I bet the shortest Gareth Ramsay has ever been allowed is a number three. But I don't think the Head will let you get it shaved as short as that again. The school hairdresser's clippers start at about number four."

"I wouldn't care," said Chris. "But I've got my own clippers anyway. I always do it myself."

"Really," mused Jules. "You know how to use

clippers? Then I think I know how to make the others stop laughing at you. Listen."

A few minutes later Jules's dad came into the room, followed by her mum with a tray of cocoa and chocolate biscuits.

"Hear you've been having a bit of bother," her dad said, sitting down beside Chris on the sofa. "It must all seem very strange, you being here in Belfast and your mum moving to Germany. Remember, she's still just a phone call away, and we're here to help you if things get too much."

"Thanks, Mr Gibson," Chris said, through his chocolate biscuit.

"Better maybe for me not to speak to the other boys about that incident this evening. Hopefully there won't be any more of it once they get to know you. But do let me know if it happens again."

"Oh, it won't," Jules said, winking at Chris. "We've got it all sorted."

Her parents exchanged surprised glances, but Chris was looking so much better that they decided not to ask any questions.

Two mornings later the Head was horrified to see the thirty-two boarders trooping down the stairs to breakfast with about five centimetres of hair between them.

"What's happened?" he gasped, pulling Jules's dad into his study. "Mrs Baird doesn't usually visit this early in the term, and she knows what length of hair we consider decent."

"It wasn't the hairdresser." Jules's dad had gone down long after lights out to investigate the scuffling sounds in the dorms and discovered Chris shaving the head of his last client by torchlight. "One of the boys had brought a set of hair clippers to school."

"Send him to me immediately!"

"Well, of course, but I've already spoken to him and confiscated the clippers." He ruffled his own rather stubbly reddish hair. "And just think, HM, we won't have to have Mrs Baird in until after half-term. We can go out and get ourselves proper hair-cuts. Our wives won't be able to insist we save money by getting ours done along with the boys."

"Hmm," said the Head, running his fingers through the few prized strands that failed to hide his bald patch.

The subject was dropped.

"You realise you've got off very lightly," Jules's mum said, when she returned from school that afternoon.

"Come on, Mum," said Jules, tucking into her afternoon snack. "Was it a master stroke or wasn't it? I've just passed Chris in the playground, playing football with Gareth Ramsay and his mates. He's the hero of the hour."

"Oh, I can't deny it worked," her mum said, acknowledging this with a hug. "But really, Jules, you do have very strange ideas sometimes!"

I *wonder* who I take after? Jules thought, finishing off her chocolate cake.

Chapter 2

Matron was having trouble with Chris's trousers.

"Just look at them," she complained, showing one pair to Jules's mum, who had dropped into the Matron's sitting room for a chat. "I've let out the waistband twice in the last three weeks *and* moved the button. What am I supposed to do next – join two pairs together?"

"Well, I can't say I'm sorry," chuckled Jules's mum. "Not about the extra work it's given you, of course, Claire, but about the reason behind it. Chris doesn't look nearly as scrawny as when he first arrived. I have to go into town on Saturday to get Jules a new winter coat. I'll phone Chris's mum and ask if he can come with us to buy some new trousers – ones with plenty of room for growth!"

Next evening, during dinner, she said to Jules, "I've been making a list of all the things I need to do in town and it's going to take me for ever. If I went in first thing on Saturday, would you mind bringing Chris in on the bus as soon as he's finished Games?"

"Yeah... OK. Anything's better than spending the whole morning shopping, I suppose."

Her mum noticed the slight hesitation. "Only if you're sure, love. I could buy you both a magazine for the bus, just in case you run out of things to talk about."

"What?" her dad snorted through a mouthful of pork chop and potato. "Jules starts conversations with the people behind her in the supermarket queue. Since when has she had trouble talking to any of the boys?"

His wife looked exasperated. "Jules is growing up," she pointed out. "Things change."

"*I* haven't changed," Jules insisted. "It's the boys who don't seem to want to talk to me any more. The ones my own age, anyway. It's like it's not cool to be seen talking to a girl."

"That will all change too in another couple of years," her dad grinned. "Gareth Ramsay and co will be rather keen to talk to you then, I'd imagine. Only by that stage it'll be too late. They'll have transferred across to the senior school and missed their chance."

"Thank goodness!" muttered Jules, looking down at her plate.

Jules's mum glared at her husband. "Just ignore your father, Jules," she said. "Anyway, you got on well enough with Chris that first evening he was up here in the flat. Almost too well," she added, remembering the consequences.

"I suppose so," Jules admitted. "But I've hardly seen him since. I hope he hasn't become like all the others."

"He's been busy." Her dad re-joined the conversation with an apologetic glance at Jules. "I've never seen a boy throw himself into school life quite as enthusiastically as he has. He's going to be a useful member of the Second Rugby XV in due course. The training he did in the Junior Cadet Corps he used to belong to has made him very fit, but his ball skills still need a fair bit of work. He's been out practising most evenings."

"I'm sure you'll get on fine, Jules," her mum said, encouragingly. "But just in case, I'll buy those magazines tomorrow. And it *is* only a twenty minute journey into town."

Waiting rather nervously in the school's blue and white tiled entrance hall on Saturday morning, Jules was relieved when Chris bounded down the stairs grinning from ear to ear.

"I've just been picked as reserve for the Seconds' away match next week," he told her breathlessly.

"Great! That didn't take long."

Chris glanced down, a bit embarrassed. "Look, thanks for your help at the start of term. I should've said so before."

"No worries. From what Dad says, you haven't had much time. Come on, we mustn't miss the bus. Mum's meeting us for lunch at one."

Just outside the front door they met the Headmaster's wife planting winter pansies and humming a tune with lots of high, complicated notes.

"Hi, Mrs Odley-Browne." Jules stepped carefully over the cluttered pile of compost, trowels and flimsy plastic trays.

The Head's wife straightened up her ample figure to look at them. "Oh, hello, Julia," she trilled, pushing back some wisps of greying hair. "Off for a walk? And... Charles, isn't it?"

"Chris," said Chris.

"Oh, of course. Well, make the most of the sunshine, children. It can't last for ever."

She went back to her pots and her humming. Jules and Chris turned down the shady drive, leaving the old red-brick school building basking in the sunlight.

"So your real name's Julia," Chris said.

"No," Jules's face reddened. "Mrs Odley gets everyone's name wrong, as you may have noticed. If you must know, it's Juliet. Worse luck."

"What's wrong with that?"

"Well, how would you like it if people kept asking where Romeo is?"

Chris burst out laughing, and ducked as Jules swung her rucksack at him.

It was one of those autumn days when the sky was almost fierce in its blueness and the sun in its brightness, as though they were both rebelling against the thought of winter. Beech trees blazed overhead as they reached the gate lodge at the bottom of the drive, a small square house built out of the same type of bricks as the school itself.

Jules checked her watch. "Quick, come and meet Molly," she said, pointing to a tiny figure raking up leaves in the garden of the lodge. "She's my favourite person in the whole school. She's lived here since the days when they had maids before the Second World War, then she married the caretaker who lived in the lodge. After he died, she was allowed to stay on here."

"I've seen her around, but I've never spoken to her," Chris said. "She helps with laundry and things, doesn't she?"

"Yes. Look, she's waving. Let's go over."

"If you don't keep the leaves under control, they creep into all sorts of awkward places." Molly had leaned her rake against the side wall of her house and come over to the hedge which separated her garden from the school drive.

"Can't you get one of the groundsmen to do that for you?" Jules said, with concern.

"Nonsense, I'm not dead yet," Molly stiffened slightly. "It keeps me fit. Now who's this with you?"

"This is Chris. He's new. Well, fairly new. He's English."

"Well, well. So what brings you over to Belfast, young man?"

"My mum's getting married again. Her fiancé's been posted to Germany. He's a soldier like my dad was. She's gone over there to get things ready."

"Well, I'm very pleased to meet you, Chris. I hope you like it here. Make sure this young lady behaves herself now, won't you?"

"Of course I will!" laughed Jules. "We'd better go; our bus is due in about two minutes. Come on, Chris. Bye, Molly!"

They just caught the bus and flopped down, panting, onto the front seat directly behind the driver. It took a few minutes for Jules to get her breath back.

"Ugh, there's my new school," she said at last, pointing out of the window. "I'd rather not be reminded of it on a Saturday."

Chris looked at her, puzzled. "I'd have thought you'd really enjoy school. Not the work, but the sport and all the other clubs and things."

"Maybe I would," Jules said, "if it wasn't an all girls' school. The other girls just seem to be into make-up and talking about their boyfriends. I hate that. At least at primary school I could play football with the boys."

"But why did your parents send you to a girls' school when you were used to being with boys?"

"It's a lot closer than the nearest co-ed school. And they thought I would get to play football and stuff back at Drum Grange."

"So why don't you? Join in when we all play football?"

"'Cos the other boys don't want me any more, stupid. It started last year, but it's much worse this term. It's like having a girl playing would totally wreck their game!"

Chris looked out of the window, taking in first the giant yellow shipyard cranes, then the impressive new buildings by the River Lagan.

"Sorry for calling you stupid," Jules said after a moment. "It's just, oh, I don't know, sometimes I feel as if I don't fit in anywhere."

"That's OK," said Chris. "You know, I felt a bit like that when I arrived at Drum Grange, but things got better."

"So they did." Jules began to cheer up. "And I'm starting the church youth club tonight. I should be able to get a game of football there. Pool, too, if I'm lucky. Sorry for moaning. How come you need new trousers already? Too much school food?"

Chris nodded. "These tracksuit bottoms are all I can fit into." He sounded quite pleased about it.

"You do look a lot..."

"Fatter?"

"No, well, yes. But I meant healthier. Didn't you get fed at home?"

"My mum went out a lot. She wasn't much of a

cook anyway. Doug, her fiancé, used to call her the Freezer Queen of Castlebridge." He laughed, but Jules noticed a slight bitter edge creeping into his voice.

"Poor you," she said, sympathetically. "I like fish fingers, but I wouldn't like to eat them all the time."

Then she couldn't help asking something she'd been wondering about ever since she'd first met him. "Why did your mum send you to school in Northern Ireland, instead of somewhere nearer your home? You haven't any relations over here, have you?"

"No. I'm not sure why she was so keen on Drum Grange. I heard her telling Doug the fees were a lot less than at boarding schools in England." Again there was a hint of bitterness in Chris's reply.

"I'm sure that wasn't the only reason." Jules scrunched her bus ticket into a tiny ball, wishing she hadn't asked.

"No," Chris said slowly, as if trying to convince himself. "She liked the way the Prep School only goes up to Year 9. She figured it would be easier for me to start as one of the older boys, than as the youngest in a school that goes right up to age eighteen. And she thought Mrs Odley-Browne sounded very kind when she spoke to her on the phone."

"I wonder if she realised how batty she is?" giggled Jules. "Did you know she used to be an opera singer? There are lots of photos on the wall in Odd Bod's study above a glass case full of all the sparkly tiaras and things she used to wear on stage. A bit like the Crown Jewels! But Drum Grange isn't such a bad place. Especially when you get picked for the rugby team."

"Only the reserves – this time," Chris reminded her, but in a much happier tone. "Hey, what's that big building over there?"

"It's the City Hall. We've arrived."

As Jules bent down to pick up her rucksack, she suddenly remembered what was inside. She pulled out a copy of *Rugby World* and handed it to Chris.

"Here, Mum sent you this."

"Wow, thanks," he said. "What for?"

"In case we didn't find enough to talk about," Jules laughed.

Chapter 3

"One more day to go, one more day of sorrow," Jules's dad hummed from behind his newspaper. It was the Thursday before autumn half-term and the Gibson family were relaxing in the living room after their evening meal.

"Shouldn't it bc the boys singing that, Dad?" Jules asked, looking up from her Game Boy.

"Says who? They can't be looking forward to the holidays as much as the teachers. Just think – no bells, boys or lessons for more than a week! This time tomorrow we'll have escaped to Ardkeel."

"You haven't forgotten you have to take Chris to the airport after the other boys leave at lunchtime?" his wife said, sipping her tea.

"No, that's why we need to get organised tonight, so we can make a quick get-away as soon as I get back."

"I was talking to Chris earlier and he seems really excited about going to Germany." Jules laid down the Game Boy in triumph, having at last got onto the next level of *Super Mario*. "It's strange because I didn't think he got on that well with his mum. He seems quite cross with her sometimes."

"She's his mum all the same and they've been separated a long time," her mum said. "When exactly is she getting married, do you know?"

"Not until Christmas, so Chris can be there," replied Jules. "He told me this half-term was too soon for her to have everything organised."

"I suppose I'd better go and start the video for the boys," Jules's dad said, folding his paper. "That should keep them busy for the rest of the evening while I pack the car."

Jules started to giggle and her parents demanded to know what was so funny.

"I was just thinking how glad the boys will be that there won't be time for Mrs Odley to read them a bedtime story," she explained. "Chris said she's been in the dorms every evening this week reading *Huckleberry Finn*."

"No!" gasped her mum. "What age does she think Chris and his friends are?"

"Anyway," continued Jules, "guess what happened last night? Peter McKnight was bored stiff, so he put his hand up in the middle of the story and asked if she had any *Goosebumps*. She looked at him, all amazed, and said, 'Don't be silly, Paul. *Huckleberry Finn* shouldn't be frightening to a big boy like you. Just pull your duvet up over your head if you're scared!'"

"Oh dear," her mum laughed. "Anyway, I could sit around talking all evening, but I really must go into the kitchen and start packing. Can you get your things together now, Jules? You won't have much time after school tomorrow."

As they all got up to leave the room, the phone rang. "Hello?" said Jules, unearthing it from under a pile of exercise books. "Yes, he's here. Cross lady for you," she whispered, passing the phone to her dad.

"Oh no, not Andrew Metcalfe's mother again!" he groaned quietly, sinking back into his chair.

In her bedroom, at the far end of the flat, Jules got out her big blue sports bag and began to pull things out of her wardrobe. A few jumpers and a couple of pairs of jeans were all she would need for a week at their holiday house in Ardkeel. Oh – and maybe some old trousers as well, just in case she got a chance to go riding with Scott and Anna, her friends who lived on the nearby farm. She was looking forward to catching up with them – kicking a football on the beach across the road from the house and searching the rock pools for crabs. But she was sorry she was going to miss two nights of Youth Club.

Saturday evening had been the high point of Jules's week since she had started going to the church youth club about a month before. The leaders were all very friendly and had encouraged her to join in the different games and activities. She already knew some of the club members from church and there were even some girls there from her school, who didn't seem so bad when you got to know them better.

At the end of each evening one of the leaders gave a short talk. Last week, Kirsty, the main leader, had spoken about some of the changes they faced as they grew older, like settling into a new school. Jules was glad to hear other people had problems with this too! Kirsty had explained how God wanted to help them cope with these changes – they only had to ask him. Ever since Jules was very small, she'd been told how important it was to make time to pray, but she knew that recently she hadn't really been doing this, apart from with Mum or Dad at bedtime. Somehow, after she'd got through the mountains of homework the teachers set, she was always too tired. Since Saturday, though, she'd been trying to remember to talk things over with God when she had a spare moment during the day. And somehow she no longer felt so lonely at school. She knew God was with her, and the other day some of the girls from Youth Club had invited her to start sitting with them at lunchtime.

Her thoughts were suddenly interrupted by a soft knock on the door.

"Mum, what's wrong?" As her mum entered the room, Jules was shocked to see tears in the blue eyes that were just like her own.

"Come and sit down, love." Her mum led her towards the bed and put her arms around her. "That phone call you took was from Chris's aunt in London. She had some very bad news. Chris's mum and her fiancé were involved in a car crash in Germany. I'm afraid it was a fatal accident. Her fiancé was badly injured, but Chris's mum was killed. Dad's just broken the dreadful news to Chris. He and the Head are in Matron's sitting room with him now while Matron gets his bag packed. Dad's taking him to the airport to catch the next plane to London. He and his aunt will fly out to Germany together tomorrow morning."

Jules began to cry as the awfulness of it started to sink in. "But that means Chris is an orphan!" she sobbed, thinking what it would be like to lose one of her parents, let alone both.

Her mum hugged her close until Jules's sobs subsided. "What'll happen to Chris now?" she sniffed.

"Will he stay with his aunt or come back to school?"

"We don't know anything yet," her mum said gently. "We'll just have to wait until his aunt gets in touch after the funeral."

"Could I see Chris before he goes, do you think?" Jules asked. She didn't know what she would say to him, but it seemed important to let him know she cared.

Her mum thought for a moment. "I don't see why not. There's probably just enough time before he leaves for the airport."

Hand in hand they went downstairs to Matron's sitting room. A bag was packed and ready beside the door. Chris was sitting on the sofa looking white-faced and stunned. Matron had her arm around him, and the Head and Jules's dad were seated opposite. Jules had never seen such a look of concern in her dad's kind brown eyes.

"Oh Chris, I'm so sorry!" Jules cried, kneeling down in front of him.

"Thanks," Chris said automatically, but he hardly seemed to notice she was there.

"Right then, Chris, we'd better go." Jules's dad helped Chris to his feet and the Head lifted his bag. Matron went downstairs with them, while Jules and her mum returned to their flat.

"I suppose we'd better finish packing these boxes," her mum sighed, looking at the things she'd taken out of the kitchen cupboards earlier.

"But we can't go to Ardkeel now," Jules protested. "What if Chris's aunt phones up while we're away?"

"The Odleys are staying at school over the

holidays. They'll be able to talk to her."

"But I still don't think we should go on holiday," persisted Jules. "It doesn't seem right going off and enjoying ourselves when this has happened to Chris."

Her mum turned Jules round to face her. "I know, love, but we have to be practical about this. There's nothing we can do to help Chris at the moment. And your dad needs to get away from school for a while."

They finished packing the boxes in silence. About nine o'clock they heard footsteps on the stairs and Jules's dad came through the front door looking tired and drawn.

"Chris didn't say a word while we were driving to the airport," he said, slumping onto a chair while his wife brought him a cup of tea. "I don't think it's really hit him yet. I just hope that aunt of his is able to comfort him. From what I gathered, she's some kind of high powered businesswoman – doesn't know a lot about children. She sounded a bit panicky about suddenly being landed with Chris."

For a few minutes nobody spoke. "Right, I may as well take these down to the car," Jules's dad said at last, pushing aside his mug and picking up one of the boxes.

"I'd better tidy up a bit." His wife also got up from the table. "Do you want any supper, Jules?"

"No, I think I'll just go to bed." For once in her life Jules didn't feel hungry.

A short time later her mum came in to say good-night. "What's happened to Chris is just so terrible," Jules said tearfully, as her mum sat down on the edge of the bed. "I wish there was something we could do to help."

"We can pray for him," her mum said, stroking Jules's hair. So they had their usual bedtime prayer and asked God to especially help Chris. On her way out of the room, her mum turned out the light, but although it was now late, Jules found she couldn't sleep. She tried talking to God about what had happened, but her thoughts kept leaping off in different directions. She remembered the stunned look on Chris's face and wondered what he must be thinking. What *would* it be like to lose your mum so suddenly – how could life ever go back to normal? And she knew it was selfish, but she also couldn't help feeling a tiny bit sorry for herself. Chris had been her only real friend in the school and now no one knew if he'd be coming back. Would she ever see him again?

Chapter 4

The school was in darkness as the Gibsons' car wound its way up the drive ten days later. The glare of the security lights anchored in the front car park only highlighted the ghostly blankness of the windows. It was as if the huge building lay sleeping, waiting to burst into life and light as soon as the boarders returned that evening.

"Oh no, it looks like the Odleys are out!" Jules glanced over at the empty parking space in front of the Head's ground floor flat as her dad swung their car into its own customary spot. "How much longer will we have to wait to find out what's happening with Chris?" Her dad had phoned the school twice from Ardkeel the previous week, but the Head had heard nothing from Chris's aunt. Jules had been hoping there would be some news by the time they arrived back at school.

It had been a strange sort of holiday. She'd had some good times riding and playing on the beach with Anna and Scott, and her mum and dad had gone out of their way to organise special treats like a meal out or swimming in the pool in the nearby town. But always at the back of her mind had been the thought of how Chris must be feeling and what was going to happen to him. In a way, she'd been quite glad when the holiday finally came to an end.

After lunch today it had seemed to take an age before they were finally packed up and ready to go. And now, when at long last they'd arrived home, there was no sign of the Odleys!

"Shouldn't think they'll be too long," her dad said, beginning to unload the luggage. "The Head will have to be here to welcome back the boys. But it's possible he still won't have heard anything about Chris, Jules. Decisions about someone's future can't be made in a hurry."

As soon as they got up to the flat and switched on the lights, Jules's mum rushed into the kitchen and flung open the cupboard where she kept her baking ingredients.

"Aren't you going to take off your coat?" Jules asked, plonking a bin bag full of dirty clothes down beside the washing machine.

"We don't have much time." Her mum was frantically sieving flour into a mixing bowl. "Granny's coming for tea, remember? I have to get some scones made."

"Surely she'd be happy with a piece of toast," her husband said from halfway up a stepladder. The clocks had gone back an hour in the middle of the night and he had climbed up to adjust the one on the kitchen wall. "We've only just arrived home. She can hardly expect you to have had time to bake."

"Darling, this is *Mother* we're talking about," his wife replied, as if that explained everything.

"I'll go down and get the rest of the stuff." Jules's dad knew that when his wife had her mind fixed on something, it was best not to argue. "You help Mum put things away, Jules."

He had only been gone a few minutes when there was a rap on the door.

"That can't be Mother already!" Her mum shoved the tray of scones into the hot oven in a panic. "She said she wouldn't be here until half past five."

Jules peered out into the hallway and saw a tall stooped figure looking strangely wobbly behind the grooved glass of the front door.

"It's Odd Bod!" she told her mum in a loud whisper.

"Ssh!" said her mum in alarm, although there was little chance the Headmaster could have heard. "Take him into the living room, Jules. I'll be with you in a tick."

"Good evening, Juliet," said Mr Odley-Browne, following her into the room and looking around as if he'd lost something. "Romeo just stepped out for a breath of air?"

For a moment he hovered in the middle of the room, chuckling with delight at his own joke. Jules's mum, who had entered through the kitchen door, dusting flour off her cardigan, hastily stepped between him and Jules's look of withering scorn. "Won't you sit down, Headmaster? Harry will be up in a moment."

"I'm glad to see someone's back on time." Mr Odley-Browne's features rearranged themselves into a frown as he lowered his bony frame onto the sofa. "I'm sure I told Matron to be here by six and there's no sign of her downstairs."

"But it's only ten past five," Jules's mum pointed out.

The Head looked at her as if she was one of his

kindergarten pupils. "No," he said, patiently, indicating the carriage clock on one of the bookshelves. "The big hand is indeed pointing to two, but the little hand is just past six."

Jules sniggered, and her mum said quickly, "We haven't had a chance to turn that clock back yet. It's so easy to forget about the hour change. *We* did when it went forward last summer and turned up for church just as the service was finishing."

The Head clapped a hand to his forehead. "The end of British Summer Time, of course! My wife must have completely forgotten as well. Never mind. It means we have more time than we thought before the boys return."

Jules was bursting to ask him about Chris, but her mum was speaking again. "In that case, you'll have time for a cup of tea."

"Yes, that would be most acceptable, and perhaps..." He sniffed the air like a hopeful, hungry puppy. "Something smells delicious."

"Do you think you'd have room for a freshly baked scone?" smiled Jules's mum.

"What? Oh, all right then, maybe just a little one." He sank back into the cushions of the sofa, looking as if he'd arrived in heaven.

"Come and give me a hand, Jules," her mum said. "Just thought you'd rather not be left with him on your own," she told her, when they'd closed the kitchen door behind them. She took the scones out of the oven and let them cool briefly on the wire rack on the table. "Put plenty of butter on them," she instructed Jules, handing her the butter dish and a knife. "Matron told me Mrs Odley's gone all health conscious and has them both on a strict diet. The poor man must be starving."

"Do you think there's any news?" Jules said impatiently. "Is that why he's here?"

"We'll find out when your dad gets up. Oh, here he is at last. Just leave that box on the table, Harry; the Head's waiting in the living room. You carry the tray in, Jules, and I'll grab the teapot."

Mr Odley-Browne wolfed down three of the scones before he at last came to the point of his visit.

"You'll want to know what the plan is for young Christopher." He laid aside his plate and Jules's mum looked relieved. Jules could tell she'd been starting to worry there wouldn't be enough scones left for Granny.

"Ms Russell, his aunt, phoned yesterday," the Head continued. "It seems his mother had never made a will, or named a guardian for Christopher in the event of anything happening to her. She'd inherited some money from her parents and that will all go to Christopher, of course. Luckily she hadn't yet remarried or things might have been a lot more complicated. Anyway, his aunt made it clear she didn't feel able to look after him. Too busy with her career, she said. She doesn't seem to know Christopher very well. She and her sister weren't close."

"Are there no other relations who could take care of Chris?" asked Jules's mum, her eyes soft with pity.

"His father was Canadian," Mr Odley-Browne answered. "His aunt believes there are relations living in Montreal, but it seems that Christopher's father had a big row with his parents before he came to England and never had any more contact with them. She's asked her own lawyers to try and trace the family, but in the meantime she thinks it best if Christopher returns here to school. His flight gets in tomorrow morning. We must all do what we can to help him come to terms with what's happened."

Jules felt her heart give a little leap of happiness. Chris was coming back, for a while at least. She was pleased for herself, of course, but she thought it also seemed the best thing for Chris at the moment. He'd made lots of friends at school and it didn't sound as if living with his aunt would be much fun.

"What will Chris do during the holidays?" her dad was asking the Head.

"Hopefully the lawyers will have some news before the end of term. If not, his aunt will just have to sort something out."

There was a click of heels on the stairs below, accompanied by a high-pitched warbling.

"My wife!" gasped the Head, giving his plate a subtle little push along the coffee table towards Jules, who was sitting at the other end of the couch.

"Anybody in?" Mrs Odley-Browne broke off in mid song and peeped into the room. "The front door was open so... Oh there you are, Herbert. I've been trying to find you to tell you your salad is ready." She looked suspiciously at the scone crumbs on the plate.

"Oh, thank you, my dear. I've been looking forward to it all afternoon." The Head quickly rose, took his wife's arm and steered her out of the room before she could ask any awkward questions.

"And what do you know, it isn't as late as we thought, so we have more time to sit and enjoy it."

As they headed back down the stairs, they almost bumped into Jules's granny coming up.

"Here I am at last!" she called, breezing through the front door. The next moment a piercing shrill shook the building to its foundations. Mr Odley-Browne had decided to test out the school bell on the way down to his flat.

"Back to the madhouse!" Jules's mum muttered under her breath. She smoothed back her hair and went to greet her mother.

Chapter 5

Jules didn't quite know what she'd expected Chris to be like when he returned to school. A bit like he'd been the night she first met him maybe, although she knew that your mum dying must be a lot worse than coming to boarding school for the first time. She wasn't surprised to find he'd lost weight again and was very pale and quiet. She just hadn't imagined he wouldn't want to talk to *her*.

"I thought we were friends," she told her dad after Chris had just walked past her on the landing, his eyes glued to his Game Boy. "But he doesn't seem to like me any more."

Her dad laid down his red pen beside the pile of English books he was marking. "It's not just you, love. He's keeping his distance from everyone. It's only to be expected, you know. It takes a long time to get over a shock like he's had. I just hope he will be able to let off some steam on the rugby field. I was trying to encourage him to come back to the team practices, but he just seems to have lost all interest."

"Have his aunt's lawyers found out anything about his dad's family yet?"

"No, it's only been a couple of weeks and it's bound to be more difficult to trace people in another country. I'm afraid it might be quite a while before there's any news. We must just try and do what we can to take Chris's mind off worrying about it."

How – when he won't let anyone get close to him? Jules wondered, going off to her room to start her homework.

The following Saturday Jules's dad was meant to be on duty, but it turned out that all the full-time boarders, apart from Chris, were going out for the afternoon with friends or relations.

"I'd really like to get down to Ardkeel to check out the pipes after that heavy frost last week," he told his wife and Jules on Friday evening. "I'm sure the Head wouldn't mind if we took Chris down with us after Games. As long as we were back in time for tea."

"And for Youth Club," Jules reminded him.

Her mum was enthusiastic. "It will do Chris the world of good to get away from school for a while. I'll make a few sandwiches for lunch and bring some of the soup Mother left us yesterday. She's made enough to feed the whole school!"

The next morning was cold and grey. Jules shivered as she got into the back of the car beside Chris. Normally she loved going to Ardkeel, even in the winter, but there were storms forecast for later and Chris was looking glummer than ever. It might have been better to stay at school, but it was too late now; they were off. At the bottom of the drive her dad stopped the car while her mum ran in with some soup for Molly, who was recovering from flu.

"Molly's up and about again," she informed the

others, getting back into the front seat. "She's had a bad dose, but nothing knocks her back for long. She's amazing for her age!"

"We should be in Ardkeel in about an hour – just in time for lunch," Jules's dad told Chris, who made a mumbling noise and turned back to his Game Boy. Jules was glad she'd brought hers too – Chris was obviously in no mood for talking. For most of the journey the only noise from the back was a series of beeps against a background of chirpy music. Jules's parents eventually gave up trying to make conversation with them and talked in low voices to each other.

As they drove into Ardkeel village, the sea could be glimpsed between two houses, grey and unusually calm, like a sheet of metal.

Jules's dad turned the car into the driveway of an ivy-covered house.

"Everybody out! First things first – let's get the fire lit. There's a bag of coal in the boot. Give me a hand in with it, will you, Chris?"

Chris helped him heave the coal upstairs. Jules's parents had bought the house as a refuge from school just after Jules was born and had set about turning it upside down. The kitchen remained downstairs, but the former living rooms had been converted into three smallish bedrooms. Upstairs they had knocked down all the walls to make a large drawing room with a big dormer window overlooking the sea.

"It's a bit of an effort to bring up coal and stuff every time we want to light the fire, but it's worth it for the view," panted Jules's dad as he and Chris hoisted the bag onto the hearth. "If we'd kept the living rooms downstairs, we'd only have other houses to look at."

Chris gazed out of the window while the fire was being lit. Downstairs in the kitchen, Jules unpacked the sandwiches and jumped up and down to keep herself warm.

"One of these years we'll put in central heating," her mum said, stirring the saucepan of soup on the cooker. "But somehow there always seems to be something else to spend the money on." She turned round abruptly. "Jules, can't you see if you can do anything about Chris? It's not good for him to bottle up everything inside him. If anyone can get him to talk, you can."

"But he'll hardly speak to me – you know I've tried."

"Why not take him down to the beach? Look for crabs, get him interested in something."

Jules thought the chances of Chris getting excited about crabs weren't high. She also hated awkward silences. On the other hand she really did want to help Chris and her mum's idea might be worth a try.

"OK," she said. "Only you suggest it. If I do, he'll probably just say no."

They ate their lunch upstairs, huddled around the blazing fire. When they had finished the soup and sandwiches, Jules's mum stacked the empty plates and mugs on a tray and handed round a bag of mini Mars Bars for dessert.

"I'd like to make a new bath panel with shells on it to replace that broken old plastic one," she said casually, avoiding Jules's eye. Her husband looked startled. "I wonder if you'd mind going down to the beach with Jules, Chris, and make a start on collecting some shells. I'm going to need hundreds."

Chris didn't really seem to care what he did, so he and Jules stuffed their pockets with carrier bags and set off across the road, where there was a lane leading to the beach. The wind had picked up and Jules's mum, with a glance at the leaden sky, had made them put on raincoats over their fleeces.

Being down on the beach always gave Jules a great sense of freedom.

"Come on! Let's skim a few stones before it gets too rough," she called, skipping over the ridges of shingle and dried seaweed onto the hard sand at the water's edge. She aimed a flat stone at the surface of the sea and it did five quick hops before sinking from view.

"Pretty poor. My all-time record is nine. You have a go."

Chris reluctantly took the stone she offered him and threw it. They watched it disappear with a loud plop.

"Oh well," Jules said, turning her back on the sea. "We'd better collect a few shells before it starts raining. It looks as if the weather forecast was right for once."

It wasn't an easy task. By now the wind was causing snaking clouds of sand to gust across the seashore, stinging Jules's eyes as she bent to pick up the shells. She turned to tell Chris they might as well give up, and realised he was still standing where she'd left him, staring out to sea. As she walked back towards him, the wind whipped a carrier bag out of his pocket. It bowled over and over across the sand and into the water, where it flapped desperately for a second like a seagull with an injured wing before the waves swallowed it up.

This sight seemed desperately sad to Jules, and when she reached Chris she saw that tears were rolling down his cheeks, mingling with the first great drops of rain.

"Are you OK?" Jules knew it was a stupid question, but she couldn't think what else to say.

"Of course I'm not OK!" Chris snapped back, wiping his nose with the back of his hand. "Would you be OK if you had no one belonging to you, if you didn't know what was going to happen to you?"

"No," said Jules quietly. "I'm sure I wouldn't." She started to walk back up the beach, holding tightly to her raincoat hood to stop it blowing back in what was now a howling gale.

"Jules, wait!" She had almost reached the lane when Chris caught up with her. "I didn't mean to bite your head off. I was just feeling sorry for myself."

"Who wouldn't?" replied Jules. "If something as awful had happened to them." The wind and crashing waves were now so loud she had to shout. "What about sheltering in there for a minute?"

Beside the entrance to the lane was a wooden shelter with a hard bench. It wasn't completely waterproof, but at least it cut out the wind. Jules had brought down some of the Mars Bars in case they'd got hungry while collecting shells. She handed one to Chris and they munched away in silence.

"I'm so mixed up," Chris said suddenly. "Sometimes I feel nothing at all, as if I've gone numb inside. Other times I'm mad with anger at my mum for dying and leaving me alone. I tell myself if she hadn't sent me away to school and gone off to Germany, the accident wouldn't have happened. Then I feel guilty for thinking like that and for being so cross with her when I first came to Drum Grange."

"I bet a lot of kids are mad at their parents when they start boarding school," Jules replied carefully.

Chris had started to cry again. "Oh Jules, what's going to happen if the rest of my family can't be found? I know I can't live with Aunt Helen – she's far too busy and we don't get on that well. I keep thinking I could end up in some children's home and then I wonder if I might deserve it. Maybe I've done something really bad to lose both my dad and my mum, and God's punishing me for it."

"Oh no, I don't think God's like that," Jules said, then stopped because what Chris had said earlier was right – she didn't know what it was like to be left all alone, not knowing who you'd eventually be living with, or where. If the same thing happened to her, she might feel exactly the same. It seemed best not to say anything else, just be there if Chris wanted to talk. She sat with him until at last he stopped crying and said he was ready to go back to the house.

"There you are!" Her mum flung the door open, wearing her coat. "I was starting to think you'd got lost. I was just about to go down and look for you."

While they were drying off by the fire, Jules's dad, who had been busy checking the plumbing, came in and announced his intention of draining down the water system in case another spell of severe weather caused the pipes to freeze. "I know it doesn't get quite as cold by the sea, but there were one or two leaks last year and I'd rather not take any chances."

"I'll give you a hand," Chris offered, to everyone's surprise.

When they had left the room, Jules told her mum what had happened on the beach. "I don't know if it did any good. We didn't even collect many shells."

"Your dad wasn't too keen on the bath panel idea anyway. Well, I did just think it up on the spur of the moment. And as for Chris, I think it may have been a start," her mum said, more hopefully.

Chapter 6

It was almost the end of term. Exams were over and the boarders were in high spirits at the thought of going home for two weeks. Gareth Ramsay had to be given detention for pinching one of Mrs Odley-Browne's tiaras from the Head's study and wiring it to the top of the Christmas tree.

"Eleanor is most distressed," Mr Odley-Browne told Jules's dad. "She felt it made a mockery of her performing days. And just when she was hoping to start singing in public again! She lost her nerve after the children were born, you know, and it's taken her over thirty years to regain the confidence to go back on stage. She was planning to top the bill at a special concert here in June – the climax of our Centenary celebrations. I just hope this incident won't have set her back."

"I'm sure Gareth didn't mean anything personal, HM," soothed Jules's dad, who privately was sure of nothing of the kind. "I'll get him to write a letter of apology during his detention and tell your wife how much he's looking forward to hearing her sing at the concert."

"*Is* he?" The Head was surprised, but touched.

"Well, no, I mean he doesn't know about the concert yet." Jules's dad suddenly sounded rather tired. "But when I tell him, he'll look forward to it, of course. We all will."

The letter had to be rewritten three times before it was judged suitable to be passed on to Mrs Odley-Browne, but it seemed to do the trick. At the school carol service, to Gareth's dismay, she came and stood beside him with a forgiving smile, her voice drowning out those of everyone around her.

A week or so before school broke up, Jules answered the phone in the kitchen.

"I think it's Chris's aunt," she whispered to her mum who was standing mixing a Christmas cake. She took the phone to her dad in the living room and came back into the kitchen holding her breath. Maybe the lawyers had found out something about Chris's relations in Canada!

Jules felt bad that she hadn't had much time to talk to Chris since that Saturday in Ardkeel. After her exams she'd been busy practising for a drama that the youth club were to perform in church on Christmas Day. Although her part was a very small one, it had given her the confidence to audition for the Junior Pantomime at her school. She had been cast as the genie in *Aladdin* and this also involved a lot of rehearsals. But from what her dad had told her, Chris had started asking every few days if there was any news of his dad's family. Wouldn't it be great if they'd now been found and he could spend Christmas with them?

A few minutes later her hopes were dashed when her dad came in looking grim-faced. "You'll never believe this! Ms Russell had booked a Christmas skiing holiday back in the summer and never cancelled it because she'd hoped the lawyers would have had success in tracing Chris's other relatives by now. She was wondering if there was any possibility he could stay *here* over the holidays. What does she think this is – a children's home? I told her she'd just have to cancel the holiday, or make some other arrangement for Chris."

"No, Harry." Jules had never heard her mum sound so firm. "I see your point, but I don't want Chris to be piggy in the middle of all this. This Christmas of all years he needs to be somewhere he feels wanted. I'd like to ask him to spend it with us. Is that OK with you, Jules?"

"As long as Chris wants to." Jules was already beginning to think of all the things they could do together, if Chris wasn't too sad.

"You're right. I'll go down and ask him," said Jules's dad, who felt slightly ashamed of his outburst.

"Jules!" Chris was waiting at the bottom of the stairs when she returned from school next day. "You're sure you don't mind me spending Christmas with your family?"

"No," said Jules. "Sometimes the Christmas holidays can be a bit boring with just me and Mum and Dad. It's usually too cold to go down much to Ardkeel. But I'd hoped your aunt was phoning with some news from the lawyers. I'm sure you'd rather be with your own family at Christmas."

"I thought I would," Chris said, "I mean I really want to find out who they are, but it might have been a bit weird spending Christmas with people I've never met before."

"Then maybe it's better you're staying with us. By next Christmas you'll probably know them really well and want to be with them. Oh – Dad says you're going over to London next weekend, before your aunt heads off on her skiing trip."

"Yes, she invited me last night after she knew she wouldn't be landed with me for Christmas. She must have been feeling guilty. At least it's only for a couple of days," Chris replied, with a trace of his old grin.

Jules had been worried Chris might be upset when he returned to school on Christmas Eve. She imagined Christmas would be one of the times you would miss your mum most. But he seemed glad enough to be back. He'd had his hair cut very short again in London and done some shopping, but had obviously found the visit a bit of a drag.

On Christmas morning they all went to church. Jules didn't sit with the others as she had to get ready for the drama, which was on immediately after the first carol. As everyone sat down after singing the last line of 'O Little Town of Bethlehem', Jules and the other actors entered through a door at the front of the church. They all carried torches and were dressed in bright colours, apart from one boy, who was pretending to be the church caretaker. "It's my job to decorate the Christmas tree every year," he told everyone, "and as you can see, all it needs now are the lights." He waved his arm towards the tree in the corner. People had been wondering why it wasn't lit up as usual. "I've looked after these lights for twenty years," the boy went on. "Every Christmas I need to check them to see if they're still working." He turned to the other actors, who had formed a large semi-circle behind him. Everyone could now see that they were linked together, through the back of their costumes, with thick green wire, like fairy lights. "I'll just plug them in." There was a plug attached to the loose end of wire dangling from the lime green outfit of a girl on the far side of the semi-circle. He lifted it and plugged it into a socket built into the stage area. There was no reaction from the "lights".

"Oh dear, that means I have to test each bulb to see which one is causing the problem." He went round each person in the semi-circle in turn and twiddled the front of their torch. The second last he tried was held by Jules, dressed in vivid pink. He pretended to tighten the bulb and suddenly all the torches lit up. Everyone clapped as the string of "lights" bowed and began to walk towards the door. It was just a pity no one had remembered to disconnect the plug. Lime Green was pulled backwards and everyone else collapsed on top of her. But this only increased the applause. It continued as the actors finally managed to leave the stage and the real lights on the Christmas tree were suddenly switched on.

There was another carol, during which Jules, in her normal clothes, tried to slip in, unnoticed, beside Chris and her parents. "No, that bright pink was more your colour," Chris said in a low voice as she sat down. She elbowed him sharply in the ribs.

The minister was now standing in the spot where the drama had taken place. A group of little children swarmed around his feet, clutching their stocking presents. "So what do you think the play was all about?" he asked them. A forest of hands shot up.

"Fairy lights," said one.

"Christmas trees," said another.

"Jesus," said a third. This was usually a fairly safe bet.

"All good answers," he responded diplomatically. "But do you know, I think it had something to say to us about our church family. Just as the whole string of lights didn't work when there was a problem with one of them, so the church family needs every one of its members with his or her gifts and talents so that it can work properly. If something is wrong with one of the members, the rest of us must try and help, just as the caretaker in the play needed to sort out the problem with Jules's bulb. That's the only way we can carry out the Bible's command to shine like lights in the darkness. So this Christmas, as most of us spend time with our families, let's not forget that we also belong to a church family. We need it and it needs us."

Jules's granny was coming for Christmas dinner, so after church her mum was in a rush to get home to check the turkey. "Well done, Jules," she said, as they walked to the car. "It's hard to keep a straight face when everyone's looking at you."

"I can't believe we got all tangled up like that," said Jules. "That's what we spent most of our time practising – getting on and off the stage."

"The whole thing was great," her dad insisted, but couldn't resist adding, "I always knew you had a screw loose!"

The Odley-Brownes were away over Christmas

visiting some of their children, so the Gibsons had the whole school building to themselves. Molly had gone to stay with a niece in the country. "This must be what it was like when the school was a private house over a hundred years ago," Jules said, as her dad unlocked the front door. "Just one family living in the middle of all these grounds."

"You're forgetting the army of servants they must have had to help them," said her mum.

"More likely than not, we'd have been the servants, not the owners, if we'd been alive then," her dad said, holding open the door. "Right everyone, up to the servants' quarters! We've a sumptuous feast to prepare for Her Royal Highness."

"Who?" asked Chris.

"He means Granny," Jules explained.

Up until the end of the second course, Christmas dinner went very smoothly.

"A lovely meal, Cathy," Jules's granny said, wiping her mouth with her napkin. "As good as I used to make myself. Apart from the cranberry sauce, of course. There's nothing quite like the taste of real cranberries."

Jules was quick to defend her mum. "Mum tried to make real cranberry sauce yesterday afternoon, but it tasted so bitter we had to throw it out. Dad nipped out and bought that jar just before the shops closed."

A glance at the thin white line her mum's lips had become, told her she'd said the wrong thing.

Her granny, on the other hand, looked like the cat who'd got the cream. "Oh, Cathy, dear, you should have asked me for my recipe. In over fifty years, I've never known it to fail."

"Why would Snow White make a good judge?" Jules's dad quickly unrolled the joke he'd got in his cracker.

By the time they'd finished laughing at the answer, "Because she's the fairest of them all!", Jules's mum's annoyance had subsided and she was able to start clearing the plates calmly.

Jules's granny was in such a good mood during the pudding course that she even complimented her daughter on the texture of the brandy butter. This time, Jules knew better than to reveal it had come from Marks and Spencer.

"Do they always get on like that?" Chris had offered to do the dishes with Jules, while the grown-ups watched the Queen's speech in the living room.

"Quite a lot of the time. Mum's always trying to prove she can do things just as well as Granny used to, while Granny still thinks her way is best. It doesn't mean anything. They love each other really. It's just a family thing. Oh no, I didn't mean..." Too late Jules had remembered Chris's lack of family.

"It's OK. What about the church family we heard about this morning? Do the people who belong to it get on well together?"

"Not always – from things I've heard Mum and Dad say! I suppose it's harder than in a real family because the people in it are even more different from each other."

"So how do you become part of the church family – just go along to church every week?"

"No, there's more to it than that. It's not even about belonging to one particular church; there are members of the church family all over the world." Jules tried to remember how Kirsty at Youth Club had explained it when they were practising the drama. "Loving Jesus is the thing that links the church family together, like having the same blood links a real family, like the wire linked the fairy lights in our play. And it's Jesus who helps us to love people who are different from us, to make the effort to get on better with them!"

"What about you? Remember that time on the bus when you said you felt you didn't fit in anywhere?"

Jules thought for a moment. Until Chris asked, she hadn't quite realised just how much happier she'd been feeling recently. "Going along to Youth Club really helped," she said. "The leaders there all love Jesus and they made me feel I belonged – not just to the youth club, but... well, to the church family, I suppose."

"Maybe it's harder to understand if you don't have a family of your own," Chris sighed, passing her a soapy glass.

"OK, you two, leave the rest of the dishes to dry and come and open some presents," Jules's dad said from the door of the kitchen.

"What did your aunt buy you?" Jules asked, as she and Chris sat down beside the pile of presents under the Christmas tree.

He wiggled his feet, drawing attention to an expensive pair of trainers.

"Cool," whistled Jules. "She's got good taste anyway."

"You mean *I* have," Chris said. "She let me loose in Oxford Street last Saturday while she was having her hair tinted."

When Jules's dad had finished distributing the presents, Chris had quite a pile in front of him. A parcel had arrived a few days before from Doug and there were also several from friends of his mum. The first one he opened was from Jules's granny. It was a knitted hat.

"I felt you needed something to keep your head warm," she explained when he'd thanked her. "With hair as short as yours, there isn't much *natural* protection against the elements."

"I don't understand," he whispered to Jules. "I've never even met your granny before. How did she know about my hair?"

"Oh, Granny misses nothing," Jules said. "Just be glad it doesn't have a pom-pom!"

Jules had bought Chris a fun book about Irish history she'd enjoyed reading herself and her parents gave him a new leather football.

"Great!" he said. "We can have a kick around tomorrow, Jules."

Jules beamed. "Oh, thanks for the chocolates you gave us. I've never seen such a big tin!"

Jules's mum was opening her present from her husband. "A breadmaker!" she exclaimed, tearing off the final wrappings. "You did take my hint for once, Harry. I've wanted one for ages. Here, hold the box while I pull it out."

When everything had been removed from the packaging, Jules's dad lifted the instruction booklet. "'Remember those golden days of childhood'," he quoted from the introduction, "'when you woke every morning to the smell of freshly baked bread...' Oh, come on. How many of us ever had that experience?"

"Cathy did," Jules's granny said smugly. "Frequently. And I don't care what anyone says. Bread from a machine will never be as good as a loaf made entirely by hand."

"Of course it will," her daughter argued. "It cuts out all the hard work, that's all. You don't have to spend ages kneading the dough. You just put in the ingredients, press a button and wait for the loaf to appear."

"Kneading," her mother smiled serenely, "is very therapeutic."

"Oh no, they're at it again," Jules sighed to Chris. "How about we try out your football now, before it gets dark?"

Chapter 7

It was hard to go back to school after Christmas. If Jules hadn't had Youth Club, and also her school pantomime coming up at the end of January, she would have felt there was nothing to look forward to. Every morning seemed dark and rainy, and dusk was falling by the time she got home from school. And if *she* was finding the start of term hard going, how much worse must it be for Chris?

It wasn't long before she found out.

"Isn't there a video showing in the Common Room tonight?" she called over to him as she waited by the car for her dad to take her to Youth Club one drizzly Saturday evening.

Chris picked up the ball he'd been kicking around the playground and came over.

"Yes, but I'd rather be on my own," he told her. "It can get a bit much being with the other boys all the time. Where are you off to?"

"Just Youth Club."

Chris gave her a strange look. "You don't know how lucky you are, Jules, living in a normal family and doing normal things!"

Jules was taken aback by this outburst. Then she had an idea. "Maybe, if Dad asked the Head, you'd be allowed to come too!"

"No thanks. I don't think all that church family

stuff is for me. Why would I want to belong to God's family when he's taken away my own family?"

Again Jules didn't know how to reply. "But Youth Club's great fun," was all she came up with. "I'd really like it if you'd come with me."

"No. Thanks for asking, Jules, but I don't really feel like it. There's your dad. See you around."

At Youth Club Jules found she couldn't join in the usual games.

"Come on, what's up?" Kirsty asked, sitting down beside her on the bench near the tuck shop.

Jules told her about the conversation she'd had earlier with Chris. "Just after his mum died he felt he was being punished, now he seems really angry with God. I just don't know what to say when he talks like that – what *can* you say when nothing as bad has happened to you?"

"I think Chris's feelings about God are normal for someone who's just lost a person close to them," Kirsty said. "He probably won't always feel that way. But even if you feel helpless to do or say anything, you can still pray for him and be a friend."

"I have been praying – a bit," Jules said. "But maybe I need to pray a lot harder."

"I'll pray too, for both of you," Kirsty said. "Now, let's go and have a game of table tennis."

In bed that night, Jules found she had a lot to think about. Talking to Kirsty had been a bit like talking to an older sister and had shown her again how important the church family was. She had always felt a bit sorry for herself that she didn't have any brothers or sisters, but now she saw how right Chris was – it was great to have a mum and dad *and* a family at church as well. She decided that every day she was going to pray three things for Chris – that he would begin to enjoy life at school, that he would find his own family, and that he would want to belong to God and to the church family. Now seemed like a good time to start.

By the beginning of half-term none of these prayers showed any sign of being answered. Chris seemed as lonely as ever around school, there was still no news from Canada, and you couldn't really tell what he was feeling about God. But he seemed happy enough when it was arranged he would spend the few days of half-term with the Gibsons.

"What that boy needs most right now is to be part of a small family unit," Jules's mum said, after settling Chris back into the spare room. "It's a pity he can't be up here more during term time, but, as Dad says, that wouldn't be fair on the other boys. Oh, Jules, we were thinking of going out on Saturday night. I was going to ask Molly to come and stay with you and Chris."

"Great!" said Jules. "Molly hasn't been up here for ages. Maybe she'll tell Chris some of her stories about the school in the olden days."

At seven o'clock on Saturday evening Jules and Chris sat watching TV in the living room, waiting for Molly to arrive. As it was wet and stormy outside, Jules's dad had gone down to collect her in the car while his wife put on her going-out face.

"More rain!" Chris said, as another wave of droplets burst against the window panes. "Do you never get any snow here? At home we'd usually have had some before now."

"Not often," Jules admitted. "There was some the Christmas before last, but that was a one-off. We had a brilliant snowball fight after church on Christmas morning."

Chris's eyes lit up. "I love snowball fights. We used to have full-scale battles in the army camp. It was the best fun ever."

"Well, it's still only February," Jules said. "The weather just needs to turn a bit colder. Listen, I think I hear Molly coming up the stairs."

"Right, do you think you'll all be OK?" Jules's mum asked, opening the front door and ushering Molly into the room. "I've left the theatre number on the mantelpiece in case there's an emergency, and there's tea and coffee and some buns set out in the kitchen."

"Get along now and stop fussing. We'll be fine," Molly assured her. "Your husband's waiting in the car by the front door. Don't make yourselves late."

When the click of her mum's high heels on the stairs had died away, Jules said sweetly, "Was there anything you especially wanted to watch on TV, Molly? It's just, I've told Chris how good you are at telling stories."

"Dear me, are you still wanting my old stories?" Molly shook her head. "Now you're at secondary school, I'd have thought you'd have more interesting things to do than listen to an old lady going on about the past."

"But the past *is* interesting," Jules insisted. "I just love history – what about you, Chris?"

"That book you gave me for Christmas was OK,"

replied Chris. "Not dull and boring like some history books."

"Molly's stories aren't dull or boring either," Jules said. "There's nothing else for it, Molly. You'll have to prove it to him."

"All right," said Molly. "As long as you stop me if you think I'm rambling on. Now then, was there anything in particular you wanted to hear about?"

"How about starting with what our flat was like when you first came here as a maid," suggested Jules. "Guess what, Chris? Molly used to sleep in my bedroom."

"Really?" said Chris. "Bet you kept it tidier than Jules does!"

"The maids all slept in the rooms at the end of the corridor," Molly began. "The living room here was the old sanatorium – where the boys came when they were sick – and the kitchen was where their trunks were stored. There were a lot more boarders in those days."

Jules and Chris followed Molly from room to room, learning about the way things had been when she first arrived and how they had changed during the war.

"An air raid shelter was built at the edge of the rugby pitch," she told them. "You can still see the rounded shape when you're close up. I spent a few hair-raising nights in there, I can tell you!"

Chris was fascinated. "You should write a book, Molly, or come and tell these things to our class. We're doing the Second World War in History at the moment. Hearing about it from someone who has actually lived through it makes it seem much more real."

"Go on with you!" Molly said, "I'm sure your teacher can explain it much better than I can." But she looked very pleased all the same. The evening flew past and everyone was amazed when Jules's mum and dad suddenly appeared in the doorway.

"You can't be back already!" exclaimed Jules. "Molly was just telling us about the Queen coming to visit in the 1950s."

"It's well past eleven," said her mum. "We didn't think you two would still be up!"

"Oh, I've been enjoying myself," Molly said, then added with a twinkle in her eye, "They say talking about the past keeps an old person's mind active!"

A couple of weeks later it was Chris's birthday. Jules was delighted when halfway through the morning it began to snow. It was the very best birthday present Chris could have had, she decided, dancing home from school under the thick-falling flakes.

In the playground she met her dad hurrying towards the back entrance with a pile of books under his coat to protect them from the snow.

"Where are all the boarders?" she asked. "I thought they'd be out here as soon as school finished."

"The Head's told them to stay inside until the snow stops," her dad said.

"But it could keep on snowing for hours!" Jules cried. "It'll be dark soon and the snow might be gone by morning. I don't believe it. It only snows once in a blue moon and no one's allowed out in it!"

"Maybe you'd have had more luck persuading

the Head than I had. Tell your mum I won't be up for a while. There's a staff meeting and then I've got to supervise boarders' tea."

He disappeared through the back door and Jules followed more slowly. Odd Bod was the absolute pits sometimes. At least he couldn't stop *her* going outside. She planned to change into old clothes and go straight out again. Only it wouldn't be much fun on her own.

When she reached the dormitory landing, she thought she heard someone call her name. Looking around, the only person in sight was Gareth Ramsay. Jules decided she must be hearing things. She began to mount the last flight of stairs, leading to their flat.

There it was again. "Jules!" Gareth now stood at the foot of the stairs. His face went a bit red as he started to mumble, "The guys have been talking about Chris. It's his first birthday since his mum died and he must be feeling a bit rough – with that and not hearing anything yet about his family. We thought we'd like to arrange some sort of surprise to cheer him up."

Jules was amazed. Gareth Ramsay was actually trying to be nice for a change. "Great," she smiled. "What can I do?"

"You know him better than anyone else. What do you think he'd like?"

"Well, what'd you thought of?"

Gareth furrowed his eyebrows. "A midnight feast maybe?"

"Bo-ring!" said Jules, before she could stop herself.

Gareth looked offended.

"Sorry," she said. "But, come on, a midnight feast in a boarding school's not terribly exciting, is it?"

"Got any better suggestions?" Gareth asked bluntly.

Jules gazed past him to the white world beyond the landing window. An idea dawned; the perfect birthday surprise for Chris.

"How about a midnight snowball fight?"

Chapter 8

"How did tea go?" Jules's mum asked, as her husband came into the kitchen later. "You didn't forget to bring out the cake for Chris?"

"No chance of that!" Jules's dad took a seat at the table beside Jules. "Mrs Odley-Browne carried it from the kitchen herself. Then she insisted on a solo rendition of 'Happy Birthday' before the rest of us were allowed to join in."

Jules made a face. "I bet Chris wanted to curl up and die!"

"I think he was quite touched, actually. She's never done that for anyone else. She even managed to get his name right!"

"Are you stuffed with cake or have you room left for some homemade bread?" Jules's mum was sawing into a new loaf on the worktop.

"Oh, I think I'd have space for some of that," her husband smiled. "What type is it today? Sun-dried tomatoes with avocado?"

"Wrong. It's cranberry and walnut. I was clearing out the freezer and found the leftover cranberries from Christmas." She passed him a plate and set one in front of Jules.

"You mean – the really bitter ones?" Jules eyed her slice cautiously.

"I think that was just the recipe," her mum said.

"Don't be cheeky, Jules. It looks delicious, Cathy." Jules's dad took a bite and his face changed. "On the other hand, maybe cranberries aren't your strong point."

"Why bother with all these strange ingredients when your plain bread's so much nicer?" Jules asked.

"To be honest, darling, I prefer your white loaves too."

"Really, you two. Where's your sense of adventure?" Jules's mum snatched back their plates in disgust. "OK. Next time it's a plain cottage loaf. I think I'll try setting the timer tonight so we can have fresh bread for breakfast."

"To remind you of your childhood?" her husband teased.

"It's funny, but I don't remember all those early morning loaves as clearly as Mother seems to," his wife said, measuring flour into the baking pan.

After saying goodnight to her parents, Jules carefully set her alarm for two am. To her surprise, Gareth Ramsay had invited her to take part in the snowball fight. "There's more chance of Chris coming if you're there too," he'd said. Not exactly flattering, but at least she was getting to join in. She tried to block out from her mind what her dad would say if he found out. He'd have a fit if he discovered the boys outside at night, and if he knew it was her idea...!

But it's Chris we're doing it for, she told herself. Surely Dad would understand that. And there was no reason why he *should* find out; not if they were careful.

At half past two in the morning Jules's mum and dad were wakened by the wail of the fire alarm.

"Funny time for a practice," yawned Jules's mum, reaching for her dressing gown.

"It's not a practice," said her husband, pulling on his trousers. "The Head would have told me. I'll make sure Jules is awake, then we'd better get out of here fast."

A second later he reappeared. "She isn't in her room."

"I'll just check the bathroom," his wife said.

There was no sign of Jules anywhere in the flat. Her mum was distraught. "Surely she wouldn't have gone down by herself! Oh dear, is that a burning smell?"

"No, I think it's just bread baking," her husband replied. "The timer on your machine mustn't be working properly."

"No, I've probably set it wrong. I've never done it before, remember. Oh where *is* Jules?"

"She's not up here, that's for sure," said Jules's dad, checking the living room one last time. "We'd better see if she's gone downstairs."

On the dormitory landing they met a stern-looking Matron.

"Oh, Claire," Jules's mum gasped. "Have you seen Jules? She seems to have disappeared."

"So have all the boys," Matron replied, pursing her lips.

Across the pitches, in the farthest corner of the school grounds, Jules dodged a snowball and rolled some more ammunition. She couldn't believe how well her plan had worked. From the moment the alarm had gone off under her pillow to the final boarder creeping out the fire exit, there hadn't been a single hitch. Peeping out of her bedroom window, she'd seen that the snow had finally stopped falling. Mum and Dad had been sleeping soundly as she'd tiptoed past their room. Down on the landing, Matron's door was slightly open, but her snores were loud enough to drown out Jules's footsteps. After the boys had been roused, they quickly pulled on tracksuits over their pyjamas and gathered around Chris's bed.

"Birthday surprise!" whispered Gareth, giving him a shake.

"It's OK, it's not a nightmare," Jules reassured him. "Are you up for a snowball fight?"

Once he'd got over the shock of being woken so suddenly, Chris was keener than anyone. "We'll have to make sure the two sides are evenly matched," he said, as they trudged through the snow. "A good mixture of ages, or it won't work properly."

When they reached the place where they'd have least chance of being heard, Chris took charge. "Don't be stupid, you can't do that," he told the younger boys, who had started to make a snowman. "A teacher might see it in the morning and wonder where it had come from. Right now, everyone, stand in a line and I'll number you off into two teams."

It would have been hard to come up with a better birthday surprise, Jules now thought happily. She had never seen Chris enjoy himself so much. And she was having a pretty good time herself. No one made any allowances for the fact she was a girl, which was just the way she liked it.

"Why's the school all lit up?" Peter McKnight straightened up suddenly from shovelling a handful of snow down the neck of Jules's fleece.

"Oh, rats! Someone must have realised we're not there," cried Gareth.

"Ssh!" said Chris. "Can anyone else hear a wailing sound?"

"It's the fire alarm!" a younger boy said in a frightened whisper.

"Oh, no; I've got to see if Mum and Dad are OK!" Jules headed back across the pitches as fast as the deep snow would let her. The boys were less eager to get back, but they followed all the same.

As they approached the back of the school, they could see a little group of people gathered in the playground – Matron, Jules's mum and dad, Mrs Odley-Browne with a purple dressing gown clutched around her, and another figure striding out from behind them.

"Boys! What is the meaning of this?" the Head thundered.

Jules looked away from her parents' grim faces. "It was my idea, Mr Odley-Browne." She couldn't let the boys take all the blame.

"Mine too," muttered Gareth.

"No, it's really all *my* fault," said Chris. "It was a special birthday surprise."

"Ah," said the Head, looking suddenly less stern. "In that case we'll talk about it in the morning. Now, has anyone found out if there really is a fire?"

"Doesn't seem to be," Jules's dad had come up behind him. "I'll just go and check the alarm panel to see what part of the school it's supposed to be in."

A couple of minutes later he returned. "Well?" demanded the Head. "Did you find out?"

Jules's dad hesitated. "The zone that was lit up was the one for our flat," he admitted reluctantly. "I'm afraid it was your breadmaker that caused the alarm to go off, Cathy."

"What?" exclaimed his wife. "I've made dozens of loaves and it's never happened before."

"Yes, but the smoke detector system that was put in last summer becomes super-sensitive at night, when you wouldn't expect anyone to be cooking or baking. I'd forgotten that when you said you were setting the timer. The breadmaker's sitting right underneath the kitchen smoke detector."

Jules's mum looked mortified. She turned to the other adults. "What can I say? I'm sorry for getting you all out of bed in this weather."

"If it hadn't happened, we'd never have discovered this little escapade," her husband said, looking daggers at Jules and the boys.

"A breadmaker!" Mrs Odley-Browne was intrigued. "I've seen those advertised on television. Could I have a look at it, do you think?"

"What, now?" asked Jules's mum, glancing at her watch. "Oh, why not? I'm sure we could all do with a cup of tea. And we might as well eat the bread while it's fresh."

Jules's dad and Matron herded the boys back to their dorms where they were instructed to change out of their wet clothes and go straight to bed. Jules followed the Odley-Brownes and her mum up to the flat.

"Amazing!" proclaimed Mrs Odley-Browne, watching Jules's mum lift the warm loaf from the breadmaker. "You must get me one of those for my birthday, Herbert. I'm sure there are all sorts of recipes for healthy brown bread."

The Head accepted his slice eagerly. "This looks fine to me, Eleanor. Ah, real butter!" His brief look of ecstasy met his wife's icy glare. "Or, more likely, a very clever substitute," he finished lamely.

Jules reckoned it was a good time to slip away. The Odley-Brownes didn't seem too annoyed by the snowballing incident. If she could just escape to bed now, her parents might have forgotten all about it by the morning.

One look at her dad's face, as they collided in the hallway, told her this was wishful thinking.

Chapter 9

Jules was grounded for a whole week after the snowball fight. Although the snow lay for a few more days, neither she nor the boarders were allowed out in it again. She also missed Youth Club on Saturday evening, which hurt even more.

"Where were you last night?" Kirsty asked her after church on Sunday morning. "It's not like you to miss a table tennis challenge."

Jules told her what had happened during the week. "I'm sorry I gave Mum and Dad such a bad fright. And I can see how it could be dangerous for the boys to be out at night when anyone could be prowling around the grounds. But Chris has started to enjoy things around school again, which is one of the things I've been praying for him. He even turned up for rugby practice yesterday after the snow melted. So how can what we did have been wrong?"

"Hmm, that's a tough one," said Kirsty. "I suppose we've got to remember that God often allows good to come of something, even when we've made mistakes. But that doesn't make the wrong thing right. If you'd waited until the next day, Chris could have had his snowball fight without risk to anyone."

"Yeah, we could have had lots of them,"

Jules agreed reluctantly. "But we didn't know the snow was going to last that long."

"It's not easy to stand back and trust God to work things out," Kirsty smiled. "The problem is knowing when he wants our help and when we should just let him get on with it."

"I suppose I'd just got fed up with praying and nothing happening," Jules said. "It seemed like a good chance to do something for a change."

"But by praying, you *are* doing something," Kirsty assured her. "Don't give up now. Believe me, God will work things out for Chris when the time is right."

So Jules went on praying. Chris was definitely a lot happier around school, especially after he made it back onto the rugby team. But as the weeks passed by, it seemed as if his family in Canada was never going to be traced. When his aunt phoned up to arrange for him to come over to London at the start of the Easter holidays, she told Jules's dad her lawyers had had no response at all to the advertisement they'd placed in the Montreal papers.

"We'll just have to make sure Chris has a good time in Ardkeel with us when he gets back from London," Jules's dad said when he came off the phone. "He knows as well as anyone that if there's no news by the summer, some decisions will have to be made as to where he's going to live."

On the Thursday before Easter, Jules and her dad met Chris at the airport and drove him down to join them at their holiday house. The countryside was bathed in spring sunshine. Newborn lambs nuzzled their mothers and clusters of gold nuggets crowned the spiky whin bushes. ("That's our name for gorse," Jules's dad told Chris.)

"Don't start unpacking yet," Jules begged him, when they reached the house and her mum had shown him his room. "I want to show you the horses, and Scott and Anna are dying to meet you!"

On Saturday, Jules's mum sent Jules and Chris to gather whin blossom from the field behind the house. When they returned, with their fingers covered in pinpricks of blood, she set a bowlful of eggs near a simmering pan of water on the cooker. "Right now, I'll put the eggs in first and you can sprinkle the whin on top. Before long we should have traditionally coloured hardboiled eggs for rolling down the hill when Mother comes tomorrow."

Fifteen minutes later Jules came back into the kitchen and lifted the lid. "They don't look very different," she remarked, bringing the saucepan over to the table, where her mum and Chris were having a snack. Underneath the soggy blossom the eggs were still brown.

"It always seemed to work when I was a child," said her mum. "I wonder if we should have used white eggs. Or maybe I shouldn't have boiled the water first. Never mind. Get the felt tips out, you two!"

Next morning they all went to the village church. Jules wondered if Chris was still feeling angry with God and couldn't help watching him out of the corner of her eye as she sat beside him on the old wooden pew. He shuffled and looked down at his feet when they stood up to sing the Easter hymns, but halfway through the minister's talk he suddenly looked up and began to pay attention.

"It must have hurt God a lot when Jesus died," he remarked to Jules as they walked back to the house afterwards behind her parents. "Maybe he does understand what it's like for me to lose my mum. I never thought of that before. Hey look, there's your granny arriving!"

Jules was excited as she carried Granny's large wicker basket into the house. Was God starting to answer her prayer about Chris wanting to belong to him and to the church family?

After lunch, when Jules's mum announced it was time for egg rolling, her mother went to her basket and produced a carton of perfect yellow hardboiled eggs.

"My neighbour has a whin bush in her garden," she explained. "It saved me driving out into the country to look for blossom."

"Oh, Jules and Chris have decorated our eggs with felt tips," Jules's mum said airily, giving them both a warning glance. "So much brighter, don't you think?"

The rest of the holiday passed far too quickly. Jules couldn't think when she'd enjoyed herself so much at Ardkeel. It was great to have Scott and Anna living so close, but sometimes they were away or busy with other friends. Having Chris there all the time must be a bit what it was like to have a brother, only better, because he was the same age as she was and liked the same things.

"I can't wait till the summer," she said, as she and Chris had a final scramble over the rocks on the last morning. "There's so much more you can do when the weather's warmer. We'll be able to swim and maybe Dad'll even let us take the boat out by ourselves and..."

"Hang on," Chris stopped her. "What do you mean *we*? *You'll* be able to do those things all right, but who knows where I'll be if the lawyers haven't found my relatives by then?"

Jules could have kicked herself. She'd been having so much fun, she'd half forgotten Chris wouldn't always be around. As the holiday drew to a close, he must have started to worry again about the end of the school year. When she thought back over the past few days, she realised that in the middle of all the good times they'd had down on the beach or on the farm with Scott and Anna, there had been moments when he'd been a bit quieter. She supposed she'd ignored them because she didn't want to spoil her own fun.

"Sorry," she said. "I didn't think. But Chris, there's still weeks and weeks before the end of term. If the lawyers keep putting the advert in the Montreal papers, one of your relatives is bound to see it in the end."

"But what if they're dead?" he asked. "What'll happen to me then?"

There was silence for a moment as they both stared out to sea. Jules felt there was something she wanted to say to Chris. Maybe she should have said it before, on Sunday, when he'd talked about God possibly understanding how he was feeling, or earlier this week. But somehow it was never easy to talk about the things that were the most important. She took a deep breath. "You know," she said, slowly, "even if you don't find your relatives, you can still be a friend of God and part of the church family."

Chris slid off the rocks onto the sand. "Maybe you're right, but I can't think about that right now. There're too many other things going on inside my head."

Jules followed him back to the house. There was nothing else for it, she was just going to have to keep praying.

Chris didn't say much on the way back to Drum Grange in the car.

"I don't know how much more waiting he can take," Jules's mum sighed, when Chris was back in his dorm and she and Jules were unpacking boxes in the kitchen. "It would be good if we could think of something to take his mind off it, something he'd be really interested in."

"But what?" wondered Jules. "The rugby season's over and he doesn't seem nearly as keen on cricket."

"The school Centenary celebrations will be coming up soon," her mum said. "Maybe he could get involved in the preparations for those."

Jules racked her brains. "Chris was really interested in Molly's stories about the school during the war," she remembered. "Could he do some sort of project on that, do you think?"

"Great idea!" said her dad, coming into the kitchen in time to hear Jules's last comment. "I've often thought someone ought to record Molly's memories for posterity and now would be the perfect time to do it. We could run off a pile of copies and sell them in aid of the Centenary Fund. There are bound to be lots of old boys who remember

Molly, coming to the special Open Day in June."

"Wait a minute," Jules's mum smiled, "I think Chris might need some help if the project's going to be on that scale."

"But I'd love to help with it!" Jules was getting excited. "We could ask Molly questions and type up the interviews afterwards. I'd better go and see if my tape recorder's working!"

Although Chris seemed really down when Jules came into the Common Room to speak to him the next afternoon, he too was soon enthusiastic about the idea.

"I told Molly she should write a book, remember?" he said.

"Well she'd never do it herself – she's far too modest," replied Jules. "But when I spoke to her earlier, she said she'd be very pleased if we did. Let's get started this evening. Only we won't have very long. She's got her computer class at eight o'clock."

"Her computer class? Isn't she a bit...?"

"Old?" finished Jules. "That's what I thought at first. But why shouldn't older people learn new things if they want to?"

"S'pose so. Tea's over at six and then I've an hour free before prep."

"That should be OK. Molly eats early. I can always stay on for a bit while you're at prep. See you at the front of the school after tea, then."

"Come in!" called Molly, when they knocked on her front door later. "It's open."

Jules and Chris entered the living room. Molly was sitting at the table, typing away at a computer.

"Just getting in some practice before my class tonight," she told them. "Take a seat. I'll be with you as soon as I've shut the machine down. It's rather addictive, isn't it?" she continued, coming to sit down opposite them. "When my niece decided to change her computer and offered me this one, I couldn't pass up the opportunity. Now I'm hooked. So what was it you wanted me to do?"

Jules had set her tape recorder on a little table between themselves and Molly. "Just try and speak clearly into this microphone here. Chris is going to ask the first few questions, as he has to leave early."

"What were your first impressions of the school when you arrived in 1938?" Chris read from the list Jules had prepared.

Molly looked at him properly for the first time that evening. And kept on looking.

Chris shifted uncomfortably on his chair. "Maybe we should let you see the questions first – give you time to think about them," he suggested, glancing at Jules.

"No, no, I just got a bit distracted. Sorry." Molly moved closer to the microphone. "When I first walked up the drive of Drum Grange, carrying my mother's battered old suitcase, I thought it was the grandest building I'd ever seen in my life..."

"I really think Molly might be losing it," Jules told Chris, shaking her head sadly. Prep was over and they were walking along the corridor towards the computer room to type up the first interview. "Did you notice the way she kept staring at you? After you left, she asked me how you were. I told her you were keen for news of your relatives in Montreal and after that she kept repeating, 'My, my – Montreal,' over and over again, as if she'd forgotten I was there. Then she totally changed the subject and asked me to show her how to send an e-mail!"

"Maybe she had some long lost love who went off to Canada," laughed Chris.

"I don't think so," Jules said seriously. "She met her husband, Sam, when she was only seventeen, although they didn't get married until he came home from the war."

They had reached the computer room. While Jules bent down to unlock the door with the key she'd borrowed from her dad, Chris examined some of the old photographs on the corridor wall. "Funny how people never used to smile much in photos. The boys in these would have been here in Molly's early years – they're mostly from the 1940s."

Jules stepped back into the corridor to have a look. "Maybe we'd be allowed to scan some of them onto the computer and use them in our booklet. We'd have to choose ones that aren't too faded."

They studied the photographs more closely for a few minutes.

"Hey, Chris!" Jules was peering at the First Rugby XV of 1945, "the Captain in this one looks like you."

"Let's see. No, he doesn't!"

"He really does," insisted Jules. "Now that your hair's so much thicker and wavier. I keep meaning to ask why you've decided to let it grow."

"I was never that keen on it short," Chris confessed. "I only kept it that way because I knew Mum had liked it."

"Well your new hairstyle makes you look like this boy's double," Jules declared. "Wouldn't it be a laugh if he turned up at the Centenary celebrations? Then you'd know what you'll look like in sixty years' time!"

Chapter 10

Spring advanced, and every week a new colour brightened the school grounds. White froth on the pear trees in the old walled garden gave way to pink cherry blossom, then fragile purple cones on the lilac bushes.

The summer exams were held earlier than usual. After they finished, the normal timetable was practically abandoned while everyone prepared for the Centenary celebrations. Displays of old photographs went up in the Assembly Hall. The choir and orchestra were constantly being called out of class to rehearse for the special concert. Through the open windows of the Head's flat, Mrs Odley-Browne's scales practice competed with the full-throated birdsong outside.

Jules found she'd scarcely a minute to herself, what with her own exams, school tennis matches, Youth Club outings, and working on the Molly project. Most of the free time she did have, she spent messing around with the boarders, who'd been much friendlier towards her since the night of the snowball fight. But she still took a few minutes to pray for Chris every night before going to sleep.

"How's the booklet coming along?" her dad asked, in the middle of May.

"Nearly finished," Jules told him. "Chris is going

to try and type up the last chapter over the weekend."

"Good, because the Head says if it's ready before the end of the month, the school will pay to have it properly printed. He thinks there will be quite an interest in it among the old boys."

"Chris will be really pleased," Jules said. "He's been working a lot harder on it than I have."

"It's great he's had something else to think about," her dad said. "If his aunt's lawyers are going to come up with any news from Canada before the end of term, they'd better get their skates on."

Open Day arrived at last. From early morning the boys and teachers were busy setting out stalls and displays at the back of the school.

"A perfect summer's day!" the Head declared, drifting around the playground, getting under everyone's feet. He picked up a copy of *Molly: Maid of Memories* from the pile Jules and Chris had just arranged on a trestle-table alongside a cashbox full of change. "A lot of hard work has gone into this. It should make a tidy sum for the Centenary Fund. Well done, Juliet."

Jules tried hard not to scowl at this last comment. Chris grinned annoyingly – until the Head added, "And of course you too, young Romeo, ho, ho." That soon wiped the smile off his face.

Just before eleven o'clock, Jules and her dad rushed back up to the flat to change. "I'll be par-boiled in this," her dad moaned, struggling into his jacket. "Do you think I could get away with not wearing a tie? It's Saturday after all."

"There won't be an occasion like this for another hundred years," his wife pointed out. "I think you could make the effort."

"I'd better go down." Jules was looking uncomfortable in the blue dress her mum had laid out for her. "Chris and I are going to do the first shift on our bookstall, then Molly said she'd take over for an hour or so while we have a look round the other things."

"I said I'd help out with selling cakes a bit later on," her mum said. "Mother has baked so many, I'll probably be there all day! See you down there, Jules."

As the door banged behind Jules, the phone rang. "If that's for me, I'm not here," Jules's dad called. "I'm supposed to be giving a guided tour of the boarding department in two minutes."

"Can you phone back later?" he heard his wife say as he made for the door, "No? All right. Just for a second, then."

"Sorry, it's Chris's aunt," she mouthed, passing over the phone.

Jules's dad groaned and leaned against the wall. "Ms Russell? I'm afraid I'm in rather a rush..."

A moment later he was standing bolt upright. "Really? How strange. Yes, I suppose that's progress. Do keep me informed. Thank you. Bye."

"Some news at last?" his wife asked eagerly.

"Not exactly. Ms Russell bumped into an old acquaintance in London yesterday. Someone who'd known Chris's father when he first came to England. She told him about the problems tracing the family in Canada. He said it would be an impossible task if they were looking for people called Jacobs. Apparently the rift between Chris's father and his family was so deep that he changed his surname by deed poll before he left Canada fifteen years ago."

"So what was his name before?" asked Jules's mum.

"This guy didn't know. Ms Russell thought her sister must have known, but she'd never told her."

"So what happens now?"

"Ms Russell is going to phone her lawyers first thing on Monday morning. It should be easy enough for them to find out from the authorities in Canada who changed their name to Jacobs around that time. Then they'll have to start searching for people with Chris's father's real name."

"Gracious! How long will that take?" his wife wondered.

"Who knows? But at least now they'll be barking up the right tree. Maybe we shouldn't say anything to Chris until we know a bit more. Right, I've really got to fly. See you later!"

Chris had changed into his blue and red school blazer and was waiting for Jules when she came down from the flat. As they walked across the playground, they saw Molly showing their booklet to a tanned elderly man with a thatch of thick white hair.

"I must introduce you to the authors," she said, as they reached the stall. "James, this is Jules Gibson and this is Chris Jacobs. Jules and Chris, meet my very old friend, James Calvert."

"What a good idea to write a book about Molly!" James shook their hands enthusiastically.

"It's a pity I didn't know. I could have told you a thing or two about her."

"James was at the school in the 1940s," Molly told them. "He emigrated when he was nineteen and hasn't been back for years."

"When I got Molly's e-mail about the Centenary celebrations, I realised how out of touch I was. Imagine Molly sending an e-mail!"

"Well, why did you put your e-mail address on your Christmas letter if you didn't expect me to use it?" Molly demanded.

"I'm very glad you did. It's been far too long."

"You've had your troubles," Molly said gently.

"I've never forgotten this old place, though," James told Jules and Chris. "I was very happy here. But I'd never have stuck it if Molly here hadn't been kind to me when I was homesick during my first term. I had quite a crush on her, you know."

"Nonsense," interrupted Molly. "I was ten years older than you!"

"That didn't make any difference. It nearly broke my heart when Sam came home from the war and married you."

"Oh well, you got over it," Molly said briskly. "This is how I remember you in those early days." She opened the booklet and held up a photograph so that it was level with Chris's face. "In fact you looked very much like Chris does now. I only noticed it when he started to let his hair grow."

"So you're the boy in the rugby photo!" Jules whistled. "See, Chris, Molly thinks he looks like you, too."

"The resemblance really is remarkable," James said in a low voice to Molly. "But there can't be any connection, surely? There aren't any Jacobses in my family, as far as I know."

"Mum!" Jules spotted her mum coming through the back door of the school with an armful of cake boxes. "Come and tell us if you think this looks like Chris!"

Her mum laid down the boxes behind the cake stall and walked across to join them.

"James Calvert from Montreal," James said, holding out his hand.

Jules's mum, Jules and Chris all stared at him, open-mouthed. Then Jules's mum pulled herself together and looked closely at the photo. "Yes, I suppose it does look a bit like you, Chris," she remarked calmly, before handing the booklet back to Molly. She turned to James. "Perhaps you and Molly would like to come up to our flat for a cup of tea at three o'clock. My husband should have finished his tours of the boarding department by then and I know he'd love to meet you."

"That's very kind of you," smiled James. "I wouldn't mind having a look around the old dorms myself."

"Something's definitely going on!" Jules caught up with Chris as he entered the Assembly Hall for the Centenary Concert at four o'clock. "I've just been up to the flat to see if Mum and Dad were ready to come to the concert and they were *still* talking to James and Molly. They told me to sit near the back with you and the boarders; they'd be down soon. Do you think James *could* be related to you, Chris?"

Chris's face was very pale. "I don't really want to

think about it, in case he's not. Let's sit over there beside Gareth and Peter."

The concert was almost over by the time Jules's mum and dad slipped in at the back, along with James and Molly. Jules noticed that James kept glancing over at Chris, but otherwise their faces weren't giving much away. It was all very well for *them*, she thought. *They* knew what was going on and *they* hadn't had to sit for nearly an hour in a sweltering hall, listening to Mrs Odley-Browne warbling arias from *Madame Butterfly*. And here she was again, taking centre-stage beside her proudly beaming husband.

"Sadly, this marvellous occasion cannot last for ever," she lamented, her best tiara sparkling in the sunlight from the open windows. "Let's bring it to a rousing climax by joining together in the school song."

"I didn't know there *was* a school song," Jules's mum whispered to her husband.

"Haven't heard it for years," he replied.

"Some of you won't know the words," Mrs Odley-Browne was continuing, "so I'm going to ask one of my greatest admirers to come forward and hold them up. Come on young Gary, don't be shy."

"Go on!" Peter McKnight gleefully prodded Gareth Ramsay in the back. "You know she means you!"

"My name's not Gary," Gareth muttered, but he saw he had no choice. He climbed onto the stage and scowled as Mrs Odley-Browne handed him a massive sheet of paper. The other boarders were in stitches.

As they all sang the old-fashioned words about being "steadfast and true to the crimson and blue," Jules noticed that James, like some of the other older men, had tears in his eyes. She wondered if she would ever feel like that about *her* school. She couldn't deny it was growing on her, but she couldn't imagine the memory of it making her cry. Maybe time changed your view of things.

As everyone emerged into the playground after the concert, Jules's dad swiftly moved over to talk to Chris, while her mum waited for Jules.

"What's happening?" Jules burst out. She was dying to know if her prayers about Chris's family had been answered at last.

"There's a possibility that Mr Calvert is related to Chris," her mum said carefully. "He's gone away now to phone Chris's aunt and think things through. But we won't know anything for certain until he's been able to contact the Public Records Office in Montreal at the beginning of next week. We can't tell you or Chris any more just yet. It wouldn't be fair to get Chris's hopes up, in case it all comes to nothing. Dad's explaining this to him now."

The rest of the weekend seemed endless. After what her mum had said, Jules felt she couldn't talk to Chris about James. On Sunday afternoon her dad took Jules and the weekend boarders down to Ardkeel in the minibus. He'd hoped a game of football on the beach might distract Chris, but as soon as they got there Chris wandered off towards the rocks by himself. It must be very hard for him, Jules thought, glancing over at him when it was her turn in goal. He'd already been waiting so long to hear about his relations, and now, just when things seemed to be happening at last, he had to endure this extra wait! She just hoped and prayed there would be some good news tomorrow.

"Do I *have* to go to tennis practice after school?" she asked her mum next morning.

"Yes! Remember, Jules, we still mightn't hear anything today. And even if we do, the news might be disappointing."

But when Jules rushed home after what seemed like the longest school day ever, her mum greeted her with a broad smile.

"So it's good news?" Jules asked breathlessly.

"I think Chris would like to tell you himself," said her mum, knocking on the closed door of the living room.

Chris and James were sitting side by side on the sofa.

"Hi, Jules, meet my grandpa!" Chris beamed, pointing to James.

"Wow!" grinned Jules, collapsing onto a chair. "I thought you might be, but how come, when your surnames are different?"

"I'll bring in some drinks and biscuits and James can explain," her mum smiled.

"Long ago my wife and I made a big mistake," James began. "We had one child, a son, who was very precious to us. We had high hopes for his future, but one day he informed us he was giving up his college course to get married. We disapproved of the girl and eventually persuaded him to change his mind. She married someone else a short time later and he never forgave us. He left Canada and that was the last we heard of him. It was only today I learned for sure that he felt bitter enough towards us to change his family name." He stopped for a moment and wiped his eyes, then continued. "I asked forgiveness from God a long time ago and prayed I'd be given the chance to make up for the mistakes of the past. Adam's gone, but now I've found Chris. I only wish my wife had lived to know she had a grandson."

"So Chris will go to live with you in Canada?" Jules was happy for him, although she knew she would miss him a lot.

"We haven't had time to make any firm plans yet," James told her. "I'd always thought about coming home for good one day. Who knows, maybe Chris will end up back here as a day boy?"

"Before he died, Chris's dad *must* have said something to his mum about wanting him to go to your old school." Jules still couldn't quite believe how her prayers had been answered. "Or else it would be too amazing – Chris just happening to end up here sixty years later!"

"I think both Chris and I would like to believe he did," James replied. "I certainly told Adam enough stories about it when he was young. On the other hand, God tends to specialise in coincidences. Either way, it's rather wonderful, don't you think?"

The next evening Molly invited Jules and Chris to join her and James for a celebration meal.

"Thanks for all your help, Molly," Chris said, tucking into a big slice of pizza. "If you hadn't sent that e-mail, it might have been ages before the lawyers found James, sorry, Grandpa."

"You must have been pretty sure James was related to Chris," added Jules, taking a slug of Coke.

"No, it was just a hunch," Molly smiled. "But I thought even if I was wrong, a trip home wouldn't do James any harm."

"We're all very glad you acted on your hunch." James raised his glass. "To Molly."

"To Molly!" echoed Jules and Chris.

After the meal James went off to his hotel, promising to visit Chris after school the next day. Jules and Chris walked slowly back up the school drive.

"I'm looking forward to living with Grandpa and getting to know him," Chris said. "But we'll be a pretty odd sort of family. We've nothing much in common, except blood!"

"A bit like the church family, then," Jules ventured. "Remember? A bunch of different people linked together by Jesus. Imagine James being part of the church family as well!"

"I'm looking forward to learning more about that too," Chris said shyly.

Jules smiled, and they walked together through the front door of the school.

If you've enjoyed this book, why not look out for these other Snapshots titles?

Flood Alert!
Kathy Lee

It was stupid, I know that now. But there was no time to think. Helpless as a bit of straw, I was tossed and shaken and dragged under water. I fought my way up – then before I could snatch a breath I went under again.

"Help!" I shouted.

"Don't bother," said Kerry. "They won't hear."

I was sinking, I was going down for the last time...

ISBN 1 85999 301 X

Lion Hunt
Ruth Kirtley

High time, short point at four.
Climb a lofty guardian;
What stops his roar?

Will Ashley and Rachel be able to work out the clues in time? And will the clues lead them to something that will save the house from being taken over by the scheming Mr Doubleby?

For Ashley especially, there is much more to this than a hunt for hidden loot.

ISBN 1 85999 412 1

Muddle is my Middle Name
Kay Kinnear

Lucy jumped back and her foot skidded. She thumped down, "Oooof" straight on to a plate of buttered toast on the coffee table. "Oh, Mum, sorry!" Lucy stood up and twisted round to look at her buttery bottom.

Lucy had promised herself things were going to change. She was going to really, really concentrate on keeping out of trouble. She was going to Become Organised, so she could make her dream come true.

ISBN 1 85999 457 1

scott bartlett